01/2022

Highlights Puzzle Readers

LEVEL P
LET'S DISCOVER READING

Bear and Friends

Fox Wants a Pet

By Jody Jensen Shaffer
Art by Clair Rossiter

HIGHLIGHTS PRESS
Honesdale, Pennsylvania

Stories + Puzzles = Reading Success!

Dear Parents,

Highlights Puzzle Readers are an innovative approach to learning to read that combines puzzles and stories to build motivated, confident readers.

Developed in collaboration with reading experts, the stories and puzzles are seamlessly integrated so that readers are encouraged to read the story, solve the puzzles, and then read the story again. This helps increase vocabulary and reading fluency and creates a satisfying reading experience for any kind of learner. In addition, solving puzzles fosters important reading and learning skills such as:

- shape and letter recognition
- letter-sound relationships
- visual discrimination
- logic
- flexible thinking
- sequencing

With high-interest stories, humorous characters, and trademark puzzles, Highlights Puzzle Readers offer a winning combination for inspiring young learners to love reading.

This
is Bear.

These are
Bear's friends.

This is Mouse.

This is
Fox.

This is
Squirrel.

Help Fox look
for a pet.

Then find the
letter **F** hidden
in each picture
of this story.

No. This is not a good pet.

Happy reading!

3

4

6

9

Is this a good pet?

No. This is not
a good pet at all.

That is a good pet for Fox.

For assistance in the preparation of this book, the editors would like to thank Julie Tyson, MSEd Reading, MSEd Administration K-12, Title 1 Reading Specialist; and Gina Shaw.

This book has been officially leveled by using the F&P Text Level Gradient™ Leveling System.

Published by Highlights Press
815 Church Street
Honesdale, Pennsylvania 18431
ISBN (paperback): 978-1-64472-459-0
ISBN (hardcover): 978-1-64472-460-6
ISBN (ebook): 978-1-64472-461-3
Library of Congress Control Number: 2021938015
Manufactured in Melrose Park, IL, USA
Mfg. 07/2021
First edition
Visit our website at Highlights.com.
10 9 8 7 6 5 4 3 2 1

Fox found a pet! But something else was hiding. Did you find the letter F hidden in each picture of this story? Now match each F word below with its picture.

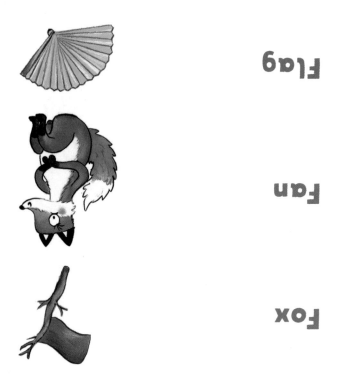

Fox

Fan

Flag